GRACE O'MALLEY

RISE OF THE PIRATE QUEEN

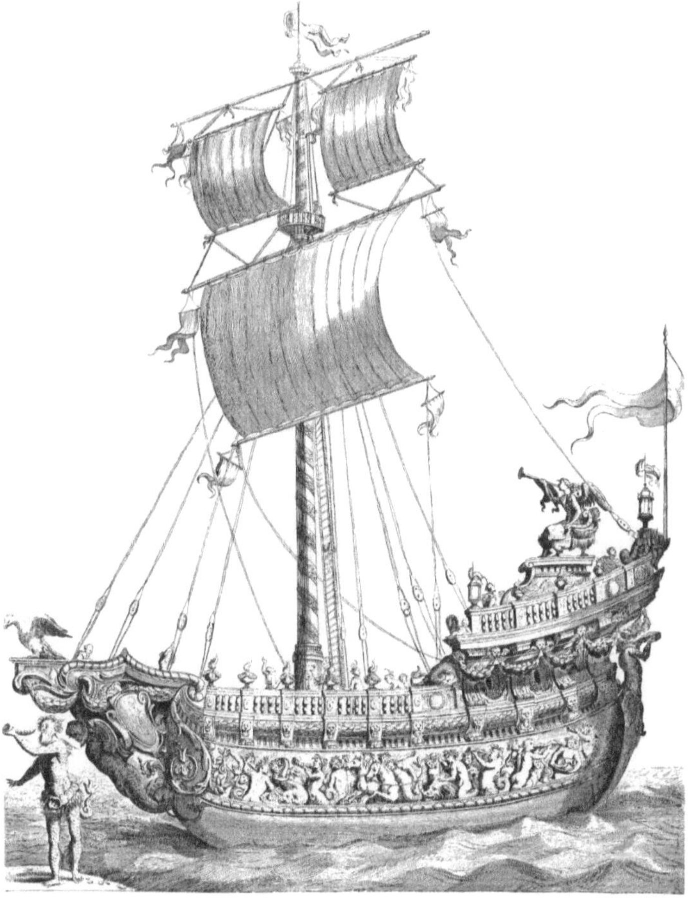

HILMARJ TORGRIM

MANDOLIN PUBLISHING
Published by the Mandolin Publishing Group

All rights reserved. No part of this product may be reproduced, scanned, or distributed in any printed or electronic form, including information storage and retrieval systems - except in the case of brief quotations embodied in critical articles or reviews - without permission in writing from the author. Please do not participate in or encourage piracy of copyrighted materials in violation of the author's rights. Purchase ONLY authorized editions.

Some names and characteristics of people mentioned have been changed, most events have been compressed. Randomly italicized words are for author emphasis only. While this story is based on the real life of the main character, it is a fictional story told through the perspective of the main character. Places, depictions, descriptions and names may have been changed for the sake of the story.

Copyright © Hilmarj Torgrim, 2024

DEDICATED

To My Beloved Granddaughter,

As you embark on your journey through these pages, I dedicate this book to you with love and admiration. May the tales of Grace O'Malley, the Pirate Queen of Ireland, inspire you as they have inspired me—a testament to courage, resilience, and the unyielding spirit of adventure.

In Grace's daring escapades and unwavering determination, may you find strength to chart your own course, defy expectations, and embrace the boundless possibilities that await you.

Chapter 1

The Sea's Child

In the year 1530, amidst the rugged beauty of County Mayo, Ireland, Grace O'Malley came into the world with the fury of a storm at sea. Born to Eoghan Dubhdara Ó Máille, chieftain of the Ó Máille clan, and his wife Maeve, Grace's arrival was heralded by the cries of the wind and the crashing of waves against the rocky shores. Legends whispered that the sea itself rejoiced at the birth of this remarkable child, destined to become a formidable force upon its restless waters.

From her earliest days, Grace was drawn to the sea like a moth to flame. She spent hours upon the cliffs, gazing out over the Atlantic Ocean with wide-eyed wonder. The rhythmic pulse of the waves echoed the beating of her heart, filling her with a sense of belonging that surpassed the confines of her humble surroundings.

Eoghan Dubhdara, a seasoned seafarer and warrior, recognized his daughter's indomitable spirit from the moment she first set foot on a fishing boat. He defied tradition by allowing Grace to accompany him on voyages along the western coast of Ireland. Under his tutelage, she learned the ways of navigation, the art of sailing, and the secrets of survival on the open sea.

Maeve, a woman of fierce intelligence and unwavering strength, nurtured Grace's curiosity and independence. She taught her daughter the lore of their clan, the ancient stories of heroes and battles that had shaped their land for centuries. From her mother, Grace inherited a keen intellect and a sharp tongue, traits that would serve her well in the turbulent years to come.

As Grace grew, so too did her defiance of societal norms. She refused to be confined by the expectations placed upon young women of her time, rejecting the notion that her destiny was predetermined by her gender. Instead, she embraced the freedom of the sea and the thrill of adventure, determined to carve her own path in a world dominated by men.

Her childhood was not without its trials. The Ó Máille clan faced constant threats from rival chieftains and encroaching English forces seeking to exert control over the Emerald Isle. Grace witnessed the harsh realities of conflict and betrayal, learning early on the price of loyalty and the importance of forging alliances to protect her family and her people.

But amidst the turmoil, Grace found solace in the embrace of the sea. She reveled in the challenge of mastering the unpredictable currents and navigating treacherous waters. Each voyage brought new lessons and tested her resolve, forging a bond between Grace and the ocean that would shape her destiny.

The salty breeze tousled Grace O'Malley's dark locks as she stood at the prow of her father's fishing boat, her gaze fixed on the horizon. The sun dipped low, casting a fiery glow over the restless waters of Clew Bay. Beside her, Eoghan Dubhdara Ó Máille stood tall and proud, his weathered face etched with lines of wisdom earned from years at sea.

"You have the sea in your blood, Grace," he remarked, his voice gruff yet filled with paternal pride. "Like your mother before you."

Grace turned to him, her eyes alight with determination. "I want to learn everything, Father," she declared earnestly. "I want to know the ways of the sea, to command a ship as you do."

Eoghan regarded his daughter with a mixture of admiration and concern. He saw in her the same fierce spirit that had driven him to defy the odds and carve a life upon the waves. But he also knew the dangers that awaited a woman who dared to challenge the norms of their time.

"The sea is a harsh mistress," he cautioned, his voice tinged with a father's protective instinct. "It shows no mercy to those who underestimate its power. Are you prepared for the challenges that lie ahead?"

Grace met his gaze unwaveringly, her chin lifted in defiance. "I am," she replied with quiet resolve. "I will prove myself worthy of the sea's trust and earn my place among its guardians."

Eoghan nodded slowly, a flicker of pride lighting his weathered features. "Then we begin," he announced, his voice carrying over the gentle lapping of waves against the hull. "Today, you will learn the art of navigation—the stars, the currents, the winds that shape our course."

Under her father's patient guidance, Grace immersed herself in the intricacies of seafaring. She studied the constellations that adorned the night sky, committing their patterns to memory. She learned to read the subtle signs of impending weather changes and the secrets hidden within the ebb and flow of the tides.

Days turned into weeks, and weeks into months as Grace honed her skills with unrelenting determination. She proved herself a quick study, mastering the complexities of sailing and navigation with a natural aptitude that surpassed even her father's expectations. Her confidence grew with each successful voyage, earning the respect of the crew and the admiration of her family.

But Grace's ambitions extended beyond the confines of Clew Bay. She yearned for the thrill of adventure, the rush of adrenaline that came with exploring uncharted waters and facing the unknown head-on. She dreamed of commanding her own ship, of sailing beyond the horizon to distant lands where legends were born and fortunes won.

As Grace approached womanhood, the political landscape of Ireland grew increasingly turbulent. The specter of English dominance loomed large, casting a shadow over the land and its people. Clashes between Gaelic clans and English forces intensified, each skirmish a battle for sovereignty and survival.

Amidst the turmoil, Grace found herself drawn into the fray, her skills as a navigator and her fierce loyalty to her family making her an invaluable asset. She witnessed firsthand the toll of conflict—families torn apart, villages razed to the ground, and a people united in their struggle against a common enemy.

But amidst the chaos, Grace's spirit remained unbroken. She stood as a beacon of hope and resilience, her determination to protect her homeland and its people unwavering. With each passing day, she grew more determined to defy the forces that sought to bend Ireland to their will and to forge her own destiny upon the waves.

As the sun set over Clew Bay, casting a blanket of crimson and gold across the horizon, Grace O'Malley stood on the deck of her father's boat, her heart brimming with anticipation for the adventures that awaited her. She knew that her journey was just beginning, that the sea held secrets yet to be discovered and challenges yet to be conquered.

For Grace O'Malley was not just a daughter of the Ó Máille clan; she was a daughter of the sea—a child of the wild Atlantic, destined to leave an indelible mark upon the history of Ireland and the annals of maritime legend.

And as she sailed into the embrace of the unknown, the wind whispered tales of future conquests and the promise of a destiny written in the salt-stained pages of her heart.

CHAPTER 2

CALL OF THE HORIZON

Months passed since Grace O'Malley's childhood days spent learning the ways of the sea alongside her father, Eoghan Dubhdara Ó Máille. With each voyage, her skills as a navigator and sailor grew sharper, and her resolve to chart her own course in life only deepened.

On a crisp autumn morning, Clew Bay shimmered under the golden light of the rising sun as Grace prepared to embark on a journey that would change the course of her destiny. Her father's fishing boat, the Aoife, stood ready, its sturdy frame testament to the years of toil and triumph upon the unforgiving waters of the Atlantic.

Grace stood at the helm, her eyes fixed on the horizon where the sea and sky melded into a seamless expanse of possibility. Beside her,

Cormac, her father's trusted first mate and a close friend since childhood, readied the crew for departure. His rugged features were etched with determination, a mirror of Grace's own unwavering resolve.

"Are you ready, Captain?" Cormac asked, his voice a low rumble in the morning air.

Grace nodded, her heart pounding with a heady mix of excitement and anticipation. "Aye, Cormac," she replied, her voice carrying the weight of newfound responsibility. "Today, we sail beyond Clew Bay. Today, we begin our journey to claim what is rightfully ours."

The crew sprang into action, their movements swift and synchronized as they unfurled the sails and prepared for departure. The wind caught in the rigging, filling the air with the familiar melody of creaking wood and snapping canvas. The Aoife surged forward, slicing through the tranquil waters with grace and purpose.

As they sailed westward, away from the familiar shores of County Mayo, Grace felt a thrill of exhilaration course through her veins.

The sea welcomed her like an old friend, its vastness a canvas upon which she would paint her dreams and ambitions.

Days turned into weeks as the Aoife navigated the treacherous waters of the North Atlantic. Grace led with a steady hand and a sharp mind, earning the respect of her crew through her courage and strategic prowess. They faced fierce storms and near misses with towering icebergs, each challenge a testament to their resilience and unity.

But amidst the perils of the sea, Grace also found moments of serenity and wonder. She marveled at the breathtaking beauty of distant lands glimpsed on the horizon, their shores beckoning with promises of discovery and adventure. She forged alliances with traders and fellow seafarers, exchanging tales of distant ports and lucrative trade routes.

Yet, even as Grace embraced the freedom of life on the open sea, her thoughts often turned to the homeland she had left behind. The Ó Máille clan faced mounting pressures from English forces, their sovereignty threatened by encroaching dominance. News of skirmishes and betrayals reached her ears, fueling a fire of determination to protect her family and her people. Never could she have known that her pleas would be the only thing that saved her brother from the vengeance of the Queen.

One fateful day, as the Aoife sailed along the coast of Connacht, they encountered a merchant vessel flying English colors. Tensions simmered as the two ships maneuvered cautiously, each captain sizing up the other with wary eyes.

Aboard the English ship stood Captain Richard Bingham, a formidable adversary known for his ruthless pursuit of Gaelic rebels and his relentless ambition to extend English authority across Ireland. His steely gaze locked onto Grace O'Malley with a mixture of curiosity and suspicion.

"State your business," Captain Bingham commanded, his voice carrying over the choppy waters between them.

Grace met his gaze without flinching, her stance firm and commanding. "We seek safe passage through these waters," she replied evenly, her voice laced with steel. "No more, no less."

Captain Bingham's lips curled into a faint smile, his eyes narrowing in appraisal. "You're a bold one, Captain O'Malley," he remarked, a hint of admiration underlying his words. "But beware—the sea holds dangers far greater than storms and rogue waves."

With a curt nod, Grace signaled for the Aoife to continue on its course, leaving Captain Bingham and his crew behind. She felt a surge of pride in her heart, knowing that she had faced down one of Ireland's most feared adversaries with unwavering courage and resolve.

As the Aoife sailed into the sunset, the wind at their backs and the promise of adventure on the horizon, Grace O'Malley knew that her journey was far from over. The sea had tested her mettle and revealed her strengths, but the challenges that lay ahead would demand even greater courage and determination.

CHAPTER 3

WINDS OF CHANGE

The Aoife cut through the shimmering waters off the coast of Connacht, its sails billowing in the brisk wind. Grace O'Malley stood at the prow, her eyes scanning the horizon with a mix of vigilance and anticipation. The encounter with Captain Richard Bingham had left a lingering tension in the air, a reminder of the dangers that lurked beyond the familiar shores of Ireland.

As the days passed, the crew of the Aoife maintained a vigilant watch, their senses attuned to any signs of approaching danger. They navigated cautiously, avoiding known English patrols and strategic points where ambushes were likely.

One evening, under a sky ablaze with the hues of a setting sun, Cormac approached Grace with a furrowed brow. "Captain," he began, his voice low and cautious. "We've spotted a vessel on the horizon. Flying Spanish colors."

Grace's interest piqued. The Spanish were known for their vast maritime empire and lucrative trade routes. Encountering one of their ships was an opportunity not to be missed. "Prepare the crew," Grace ordered, her voice tinged with excitement. "We'll approach cautiously. I want to know who they are and what business brings them to these waters."

The Aoife altered its course, closing the distance between them and the Spanish vessel. As they drew nearer, Grace observed the sleek lines of the galleon, its flags fluttering in the breeze. The Spaniards, renowned for their maritime prowess, were quick to spot the approach of the Irish ship.

Aboard the galleon, Captain Diego Ramirez surveyed the scene with a mixture of curiosity and caution. He was a seasoned mariner, his weathered features and confident bearing a testament to years spent navigating the unpredictable waters of the Atlantic.

"Identify yourselves!" Captain Ramirez called out in Spanish, his voice carrying over the water.

Grace stepped forward, her presence commanding despite her youth. "I am Grace O'Malley, Captain of the Aoife," she replied in clear Spanish, her accent betraying her Irish heritage. "We mean no harm. We seek safe passage and perhaps a chance to trade."

Captain Ramirez regarded her with a shrewd gaze, assessing the Irish captain and her crew. "I have heard of you, Grace O'Malley," he remarked, a note of respect in his voice. "They say you are a formidable sailor and a fierce protector of your homeland."

Grace inclined her head in acknowledgment. "And I have heard tales of the Spanish fleet's exploits in these waters," she replied evenly, her eyes locked with his. "Perhaps there is an opportunity for mutual benefit."

A smile tugged at the corners of Captain Ramirez's lips. "Perhaps indeed," he agreed, his tone warm with camaraderie. "Come aboard, Captain O'Malley. Let us discuss the terms of our potential alliance."

With cautious optimism, Grace and a select few of her crew boarded the Spanish galleon. They were greeted warmly by Captain Ramirez and his officers, the atmosphere aboard the ship buzzing with the promise of new beginnings and shared ventures.

Over a feast of salted fish, olives, and wine, Grace and Captain Ramirez exchanged tales of their respective journeys and triumphs. They spoke of the challenges faced as seafarers, the dangers of piracy and privateers, and the thrill of discovering new lands and cultures.

As the evening wore on, Grace found herself drawn to Captain Ramirez's easy charm and depth of knowledge. He spoke passionately of his homeland in Spain, of its rich history and vibrant cities. In turn, Grace regaled him with stories of Ireland—the emerald hills, the ancient castles, and the resilient spirit of its people.

Underneath the camaraderie and business discussions, a subtle undercurrent of attraction simmered between them. Grace felt a flutter of excitement in her chest, a sensation she had rarely experienced amidst the harsh realities of life at sea.

Later that night, as the stars painted patterns across the velvet sky, Grace stood at the railing of the Spanish galleon, her thoughts consumed by the enigmatic Captain Ramirez. She gazed out over the moonlit waters, the rhythmic pulse of the ocean a soothing balm to her restless spirit.

"Captain O'Malley," a voice called softly from behind her.

Grace turned to find Captain Ramirez approaching, his silhouette outlined against the shimmering backdrop of the night. "Captain Ramirez," she replied, her voice betraying a hint of uncertainty.

He stopped before her, his eyes locking onto hers with an intensity that sent a shiver down her spine. "Grace," he murmured, his voice low and intimate. "I sense a kindred spirit in you—a woman of courage and conviction, unafraid to defy the odds."

Grace met his gaze, her heart racing with a mixture of apprehension and longing. "I am bound by duty and honor, Captain Ramirez," she replied softly, her words a gentle plea for understanding.

He reached out, his hand brushing against hers with a touch as light as the breeze. "As am I," he murmured, his voice tinged with longing. "But tonight, let us set aside duty and honor. Let us embrace the fleeting moments we are granted."

In that moonlit embrace, beneath a tapestry of stars and the whisper of the sea, Grace O'Malley surrendered to the allure of forbidden desire. For in Captain Diego Ramirez, she found not only a kindred spirit but a catalyst for change—a man who challenged her to envision a future beyond the confines of tradition and duty.

CHAPTER 4

SHADOWS OF INTRIGUE

In the wake of their encounter with Captain Diego Ramirez and the Spanish galleon, the Aoife sailed southward along the rugged coast of Connacht. Grace O'Malley stood at the helm, her mind awash with conflicting emotions. The memory of her night with Captain Ramirez lingered like a bittersweet melody, filling her heart with both exhilaration and trepidation.

Cormac approached her, his presence a reassuring anchor amidst the swirling currents of her thoughts. "Captain," he began, his voice gentle yet probing. "You seem distant. Is something troubling you?"

Grace turned to him, her expression guarded yet tinged with vulnerability. "It's nothing, Cormac," she replied evasively, her fingers tightening around the wooden wheel. "Just... thoughts of what lies ahead."

Cormac studied her for a moment, his keen eyes betraying his concern. He knew Grace better than anyone—her fierce determination, her unwavering loyalty to her homeland, and the steely resolve that had propelled her to become the formidable captain she was.

"Grace," he began softly, choosing his words with care. "You have always been guided by your instincts. But remember, not all paths lead where we expect them to."

Grace met his gaze, a flicker of uncertainty shadowing her features. "What do you mean, Cormac?" she asked, her voice edged with apprehension.

He sighed, his expression troubled. "I mean Captain Ramirez," he replied carefully. "He is a Spaniard—a foreigner with his own ambitions and loyalties. Can we trust him, truly?"

The question hung heavy in the air, its implications weighing on Grace's heart. She knew Cormac spoke from a place of loyalty and concern, his words a reminder of the complexities that lay beneath the surface of their newfound alliance with the Spanish.

"I don't know," Grace admitted quietly, her gaze drifting out to sea where the horizon blurred into the distant unknown. "But we need allies, Cormac. The English grow stronger with each passing day, and our people suffer under their tyranny."

Cormac nodded slowly, his expression thoughtful. "True enough," he conceded. "But trust must be earned, Grace. We cannot afford to be blinded by the promise of alliances without understanding the motives that drive them."

Grace sighed, her shoulders tense with the weight of responsibility. She knew Cormac spoke with wisdom born of experience, his caution a stark contrast to her own impulsive nature. But deep down, she also knew that the bond she shared with Captain Ramirez went beyond mere alliance—it was forged in the crucible of shared ambition and mutual respect.

As the Aoife sailed onward, Grace wrestled with her conflicting emotions. She found herself drawn to Captain Ramirez's charisma and steadfastness, his presence a source of strength in the face of uncertainty. Yet, beneath the allure of their burgeoning connection lay the shadows of intrigue and unanswered questions.

Days turned into weeks as the Aoife continued its voyage along the western coast of Ireland. They encountered fellow Gaelic clans, forging alliances and strengthening bonds in preparation for the inevitable clash with English forces. News of their exploits spread like wildfire, sparking hope among the oppressed and fear among their adversaries.

One stormy night, as the Aoife sought shelter in a secluded cove off the coast of Clare, Grace found herself haunted by restless dreams. Visions of battles fought and lost, of faces she had sworn to protect, flickered through her mind like shadows dancing on the edge of consciousness.

She paced the deck, the wind whipping through her hair and the crash of waves echoing in her ears. The storm mirrored the turmoil within her heart, its fury a reflection of the tumultuous path she had chosen to tread.

"Grace," a voice called softly from behind her.

She turned to find Cormac standing there, his weathered face etched with concern. "Cormac," she greeted him quietly, her voice hoarse with fatigue. "Is everything alright?"

He approached her, his gaze steady and unwavering. "You've been distant lately," he observed gently. "Ever since Captain Ramirez..."

Grace sighed, her shoulders sagging under the weight of unspoken doubts. "I don't know what to do, Cormac," she admitted, her voice barely above a whisper. "Part of me wants to trust him, to believe in what we can accomplish together. But another part fears the consequences of misplaced trust."

Cormac placed a comforting hand on her shoulder, his touch grounding her amidst the storm raging both outside and within. "Trust your instincts, Grace," he counseled softly. "You have a keen sense of right and wrong, of loyalty and honor. Let them guide you."

She nodded slowly, a sense of clarity settling over her like a mantle of peace. "Thank you, Cormac," she murmured gratefully, her gaze turning once more to the turbulent sea. "I needed to hear that."

As the storm raged on, Grace O'Malley stood at the helm of the Aoife, her resolve renewed and her spirit fortified. The path ahead was fraught with uncertainty and peril, but she knew that with courage and determination, she would navigate the treacherous waters that lay ahead.

CHAPTER 5

BONDS OF ALLEGIANCE

The morning sun bathed the cliffs of Clare in a golden hue as Grace O'Malley stood on the deck of the Aoife, her mind clear and resolute. The storm had passed, leaving behind a tranquil sea and a sense of renewed purpose within her heart.

She called for Cormac and gathered her most trusted crewmates for a council on deck. "We must decide our next course of action," Grace announced, her voice steady and commanding. "The English grow bolder, and our people suffer under their tyranny. We need allies—strong alliances that will bolster our defenses and strengthen our resolve."

Cormac nodded in agreement, his expression grave yet determined. "Aye, Captain," he replied. "But where do we turn? The clans of

Connacht are wary, and our options are limited."

Grace surveyed her crew, their faces reflecting a mixture of anticipation and apprehension. "We have forged a tentative alliance with Captain Ramirez and the Spanish," she began, her voice measured yet tinged with optimism. "Their fleet patrols these waters, a formidable force against our common enemy."

There was a murmur of agreement among the crew, their eyes alight with renewed hope. The prospect of joining forces with the Spanish offered a glimmer of opportunity in the face of overwhelming odds.

"Prepare the Aoife," Grace commanded, her voice ringing with authority. "We sail for Spanish waters. We will seek Captain Ramirez and discuss the terms of our alliance."

The crew sprang into action, their movements swift and purposeful as they readied the ship for departure. The sails were unfurled, the rigging inspected, and provisions stocked for the journey ahead. Grace watched with pride as her crew worked in harmony, their loyalty to her and their shared cause a testament to the bonds that united them.

As the Aoife sailed southward, Grace's thoughts turned to Captain Diego Ramirez and the enigmatic connection that had sparked between them. She recalled their conversations beneath the stars, their shared dreams of freedom and justice for their people. Despite Cormac's warnings and the shadow of uncertainty that lingered, Grace couldn't deny the pull she felt toward the charismatic Spanish captain.

Days passed in a blur of open seas and starlit nights. The Aoife navigated through calm waters and gentle currents, its bow pointed toward the distant shores of Spain. Along the way, they encountered merchant vessels and fellow seafarers, exchanging news of distant lands and trading goods in a show of camaraderie that transcended borders.

Finally, after weeks of sailing, the Aoife approached the bustling port city of Cádiz. Grace's heart quickened with anticipation as she beheld the towering masts and bustling activity of the Spanish fleet anchored in the harbor. She ordered the crew to prepare for docking, eager to reunite with Captain Ramirez and solidify their alliance.

Once ashore, Grace and a select few of her crew made their way through the narrow streets of Cádiz, guided by locals to the grand villa where Captain Ramirez had established his headquarters. The air was alive with the scent of salt and spices, the sounds of merchants haggling and children playing echoing through the sun-dappled alleys.

At last, they arrived at the villa—a sprawling estate overlooking the azure waters of the Mediterranean. Grace took a moment to steady herself, her heart pounding with a mix of nerves and anticipation. With a deep breath, she entered the courtyard where Captain Ramirez awaited her.

He turned at the sound of approaching footsteps, his expression a mixture of surprise and delight. "Grace," he greeted her warmly, his voice carrying over the gentle rustle of palm leaves in the breeze. "I had not expected to see you so soon."

Grace met his gaze, her own eyes bright with determination. "Captain Ramirez," she replied, her voice tinged with respect. "We have much to discuss—our alliance, our goals, and the future of our people."

Captain Ramirez nodded, his features serious yet tinged with a hint of admiration. "Indeed," he agreed, gesturing for Grace to join him at a shaded table overlooking the sea. "But first, let us celebrate the journey that has brought us together. To new beginnings and shared victories."

They shared a meal of fresh seafood and local wine, their conversation weaving between strategy and personal anecdotes. Grace found herself drawn to Captain Ramirez's intelligence and wit, his passion for justice and freedom echoing her own.

As the sun dipped below the horizon, casting a tapestry of colors across the sky, Grace and Captain Ramirez forged a bond of allegiance and mutual respect. They spoke of the challenges ahead, the risks they would face, and the sacrifices they were willing to make for their shared cause.

In that moment, amidst the beauty of a Mediterranean sunset and the promise of a future defined by unity and strength, Grace O'Malley knew that she had found not only an ally in Captain Diego Ramirez but a partner who believed in her vision and shared her unwavering commitment to freedom and justice.

And as they gazed out over the shimmering waters of Cádiz harbor, their hearts beat in rhythm with the ebb and flow of the tide—a testament to the enduring power of courage, camaraderie, and the bonds that transcend borders and seas.

CHAPTER 6

Shadows of Betrayal

The alliance with Captain Diego Ramirez and the Spanish fleet proved to be a turning point for Grace O'Malley and the crew of the Aoife. As they sailed alongside their newfound allies, their confidence grew, bolstered by the strength of their combined forces and shared determination to resist English encroachment.

In the weeks that followed their meeting in Cádiz, Grace and Captain Ramirez worked tirelessly to solidify their alliance. They strategized, exchanged intelligence on English movements, and forged agreements to support each other in times of need. The Spanish provided vital supplies and reinforcements, while Grace's crew offered their expertise in navigating the treacherous waters of the Irish coast.

Amidst the flurry of preparations and strategic discussions, Grace found herself increasingly drawn to Captain Ramirez's company. They shared moments of camaraderie and shared purpose, their bond deepening with each passing day. Yet, beneath the surface of their alliance, shadows of doubt and uncertainty lingered.

One evening, as they stood together on the deck of the Aoife, watching the sun sink below the horizon, Grace broached the topic that had been weighing on her mind. "Diego," she began softly, her voice carrying the weight of unspoken questions. "Tell me about your ambitions for Spain and our alliance."

Captain Ramirez turned to her, his gaze steady and unreadable. "Grace," he replied carefully, choosing his words with caution. "My ambitions are simple—to safeguard Spanish interests and protect our shared values of freedom and justice. Our alliance is based on mutual respect and a common enemy."

Grace studied him intently, searching his face for any hint of deception. "And what of your loyalty to Spain?" she pressed, her voice tinged with concern. "Will it ever conflict with our goals for Ireland?"

There was a moment of silence between them, the only sound the gentle lapping of waves against the hull of the ship. Captain Ramirez sighed, his expression conflicted yet resolute. "Grace," he began earnestly, reaching out to gently cup her cheek. "I am committed to our cause—to your cause. My loyalty lies with you and the fight for justice against English tyranny."

Grace leaned into his touch, her heart fluttering with a mixture of relief and trepidation. She wanted to believe in Captain Ramirez, to trust in their alliance and the future they were forging together. Yet, Cormac's warnings echoed in the recesses of her mind, reminding her of the dangers of misplaced trust and the shadows of betrayal that lurked in the periphery.

As the days turned into weeks, Grace and Captain Ramirez led their combined forces in a series of successful raids against English outposts along the Irish coast. They struck swiftly and decisively, reclaiming territory and bolstering the morale of their people. Each victory strengthened their resolve and solidified their reputation as formidable adversaries to English dominance.

But amidst the triumphs and camaraderie, tensions simmered beneath the surface. Rumors spread among the crew of the Aoife—whispers of spies and double agents, of secret alliances and hidden agendas. Grace remained vigilant, her instincts sharpened by years of navigating the treacherous waters of political intrigue and betrayal.

One night, as she stood alone on the deck of the Aoife, gazing out over the moonlit sea, Grace sensed a presence behind her. She turned to find Cormac approaching, his expression grave and troubled.

"Captain," he began quietly, his voice barely above a whisper. "I have troubling news."

Grace's heart clenched with apprehension. "What is it, Cormac?" she asked, her voice steady despite the rising tide of unease within her.

He hesitated for a moment, his gaze fixed on the distant horizon. "There are whispers among the crew," he confessed reluctantly. "Whispers of a plot—a betrayal from within our ranks."

Grace's blood ran cold, her mind racing with the implications of Cormac's words. "Who?" she demanded, her voice sharp with urgency. "Who would betray us?"

Cormac shook his head, his jaw clenched with frustration. "I do not know," he admitted, his voice tinged with regret. "But there are murmurs of a traitor among us, feeding information to the English."

Grace's hands clenched into fists at her sides, her thoughts racing as she considered the gravity of the situation. The success of their alliance with the Spanish—and the safety of their people—depended on secrecy and trust. A betrayal from within could jeopardize everything they had worked so hard to achieve.

"We must uncover the truth," Grace declared firmly, her jaw set with determination. "We cannot afford to overlook this threat, Cormac. Our lives and the future of Ireland hang in the balance."

Cormac nodded solemnly, his expression mirroring Grace's steely resolve. "Aye, Captain," he agreed. "We will root out the traitor and ensure that justice is served."

As the moon cast its silvery glow over the restless sea, Grace O'Malley vowed to confront the shadows of betrayal that threatened to unravel their alliance and her dreams of a free and prosperous Ireland. She would uncover the truth, no matter the cost, and safeguard the bonds of allegiance that held their destiny in the balance.

Chapter 7

Shadows Unveiled

The Aoife sailed on, cutting through the waves with purposeful determination. The winds whispered secrets of impending storms, yet Grace O'Malley's mind remained fixed on the unsettling news of betrayal within her ranks. As captain, she felt the weight of responsibility heavy upon her shoulders, knowing that the security of their alliance with Captain Diego Ramirez and the Spanish fleet hung in the balance.

On deck, tensions simmered among the crew. Whispers grew louder, suspicions deepened, and trust became a fragile commodity. Grace observed her crew with a keen eye, searching for any signs of deceit or treachery amidst the familiar faces she had come to rely upon.

Cormac approached her one evening, his expression grave yet resolute. "Captain," he began, his voice low and urgent. "We must act swiftly. The whispers have grown louder, and trust among the crew is faltering."

Grace nodded in agreement, her jaw set with determination. "Gather our most trusted allies," she instructed Cormac. "We will convene in the captain's quarters. We must uncover the truth before it's too late."

Under the cover of darkness, Grace and her closest advisors met in the dimly lit quarters of the Aoife. The air was thick with tension as they discussed the rumors of betrayal and strategized their next move.

"We cannot afford to confront Captain Ramirez without concrete evidence," Cormac advised, his voice tinged with caution. "Accusations of espionage could irreparably damage our alliance and play into the hands of our true enemies."

Grace nodded thoughtfully, weighing Cormac's words against the urgency of the situation. "Agreed," she replied evenly. "But we must proceed with caution. We need to gather intelligence, discreetly uncover the identity of the traitor, and assess the extent of the damage they may have caused."

They devised a plan to discreetly observe the interactions among the crew, monitor communications, and search for any signs of suspicious behavior. Each member of the crew was scrutinized, their actions and allegiances questioned under the veil of secrecy.

Days turned into weeks as Grace and her allies worked tirelessly to unravel the web of deception that threatened their alliance. They followed leads, pieced together fragmented clues, and interrogated suspects in the dead of night.

One evening, as Grace walked along the deserted deck of the Aoife, her thoughts consumed by the weight of their mission, she heard footsteps approaching from behind. She turned to find Captain Ramirez standing there, his expression unreadable in the dim glow of the lanterns.

"Grace," he greeted her quietly, his voice tinged with concern. "I have noticed a shift in our alliance. Tell me, is everything well?"

Grace regarded him cautiously, her mind racing with the suspicion and uncertainty that clouded her thoughts. "Captain Ramirez," she began carefully, choosing her words with caution. "There have been... concerns among my crew. Whispers of betrayal, of secrets shared with our enemies."

Captain Ramirez's brow furrowed with concern. "I assure you, Grace," he replied earnestly. "I am committed to our cause—to your cause. I would never betray your trust or jeopardize our alliance."

Grace studied him intently, searching his face for any hint of deception. "I want to believe you, Diego," she admitted softly, her voice tinged with vulnerability. "But the stakes are too high, and the shadows of betrayal loom over us."

Captain Ramirez reached out, his hand gently cupping her cheek. "Trust in me, Grace," he urged earnestly, his gaze unwavering. "I swear to you—I am your ally, your friend, and your partner in this fight for freedom."

In that moment, beneath the starlit sky and the vast expanse of the ocean, Grace O'Malley felt a flicker of hope amidst the uncertainty that clouded their path. She wanted to believe in Captain Ramirez, to trust in their alliance and the bond that had grown between them.

The shadows of betrayal still lurked in the shadows, waiting to be unveiled, and the fate of their alliance—and the future of Ireland—hung in the balance.

Chapter 8

Clash of Blades

The tension aboard the Aoife was palpable as Grace O'Malley and Captain Diego Ramirez navigated the delicate balance of trust and suspicion. Days turned into nights filled with strategizing, surveilling, and searching for the elusive traitor among their ranks. Meanwhile, their alliance with the Spanish fleet continued to hold, bolstered by successful raids on English vessels and the shared determination to defy oppression.

One moonlit night, as the Aoife sailed along the western coast of Ireland, a cry pierced the silence. Grace bolted upright in her quarters, her senses on high alert. She reached for her cutlass and rushed on deck, where chaos had erupted among the crew.

In the flickering light of the lanterns, Grace saw two figures locked in a deadly dance of steel. It was Cormac—her trusted friend and second-in-command—pitted against another crew member, their faces contorted with rage and desperation.

Without hesitation, Grace lunged into action, her cutlass gleaming in the moonlight as she deflected blows and parried strikes. She fought with the skill and ferocity that had earned her the reputation as the Pirate Queen of Ireland, her focus unwavering as she sought to restore order and uncover the truth.

"Cormac!" she called out, her voice cutting through the chaos. "Stand down!"

But Cormac's assailant pressed on, driven by a relentless fury that defied reason. Their swords clashed with a thunderous ring, the sound echoing across the deck as they circled each other in a deadly dance of blades.

Grace moved with calculated precision, her movements fluid and controlled. She anticipated each strike, countering with skillful maneuvers honed through years of training and countless battles. Yet, her heart clenched with the realization that this fight was not just about quelling a mutiny—it was a battle for the soul of their crew and the security of their alliance.

As the fight intensified, Grace glimpsed Captain Ramirez at the edge of the fray, his expression a mask of concern and determination. Their eyes met briefly, a silent exchange of understanding and resolve amidst the chaos that engulfed them.

With a swift and decisive move, Grace disarmed Cormac's assailant, sending his sword clattering to the deck. She held her cutlass at his throat, her breath coming in ragged gasps as she stared into eyes filled with defiance and desperation.

"Who sent you?" Grace demanded, her voice cutting through the tension like a blade. "Who betrayed us?"

The crew member sneered, his lips twisting into a scornful grin. "You think you can trust the Spaniard?" he spat, his voice thick with bitterness. "He's playing you, Grace—playing all of us. You'll see."

Before Grace could press further, he wrenched himself free and lunged for his fallen sword. In an instant, he was on his feet, ready to resume the fight with renewed ferocity.

But before he could strike, Captain Ramirez intervened, his own blade flashing in the moonlight as he stepped between Grace and the assailant. "Enough!" he commanded, his voice ringing with authority. "Stand down, both of you."

The assailant hesitated, caught between defiance and resignation. He glanced at Grace and then at Captain Ramirez, weighing his options in the tense silence that enveloped them.

"Enough blood has been spilled tonight," Captain Ramirez continued, his gaze unwavering. "We are allies in this fight, not enemies."

Slowly, reluctantly, the assailant lowered his sword and dropped to his knees, his shoulders slumped with defeat. Grace watched him closely, her mind racing with conflicting emotions as she processed the implications of his words.

"Lock him in chains," she ordered, her voice steady despite the turmoil within her. "Lock him away until we reach port. We will interrogate him further."

As the crew subdued the assailant and secured him below deck, Grace turned to Captain Ramirez, her expression troubled yet resolute. "Diego," she began quietly, her voice tinged with uncertainty. "What he said... about you..."

Captain Ramirez met her gaze, his own eyes filled with a mixture of sorrow and determination. "I swear to you, Grace," he replied earnestly, his voice low and intense. "I am loyal to our cause, to our alliance. I will prove it to you."

Grace nodded slowly, her heart heavy with the weight of doubt and mistrust. "I want to believe you, Diego," she admitted softly, her voice tinged with vulnerability. "But we cannot ignore the warning signs. We must proceed with caution."

Captain Ramirez reached out, his hand gently clasping hers. "I understand," he murmured, his touch a reassuring anchor amidst the storm that raged within them. "Trust takes time, Grace. But I am here, by your side, every step of the way."

CHAPTER 9

WINDS OF CHANGE

The winds shifted, carrying with them a sense of unease as the Aoife continued its journey along the rugged Irish coastline. Grace O'Malley stood at the bow of the ship, her gaze fixed on the horizon where the sea met the sky. The events of recent days weighed heavily on her mind—the betrayal within their ranks, the whispers of intrigue, and the fragile trust that now hung in the balance.

Below deck, the crew moved with quiet efficiency, their camaraderie tempered by the shadow of suspicion that had taken root among them. Grace knew that restoring trust and unity was essential if they were to maintain their strength against the relentless forces of English oppression.

In the captain's quarters, Grace met with Cormac and her closest advisors to discuss their next course of action. "We need to root out the traitors," she declared firmly, her voice resonating with determination. "We cannot afford to underestimate the threats that surround us."

Cormac nodded in agreement, his expression grim yet resolute. "Aye, Captain," he replied. "But how do we proceed? The traitor could be anyone—someone we trust implicitly."

Grace considered his words carefully, her mind racing with possibilities. "We will continue to gather intelligence," she decided, her tone decisive. "We will watch, listen, and wait for the right moment to strike."

As they deliberated their strategy, a commotion erupted on deck—a cry of alarm followed by the urgent clang of bells. Grace and Cormac exchanged a swift glance before rushing to join the crew on deck.

"What is it?" Grace demanded as she emerged into the chaos that greeted her. A crew member pointed toward the horizon, where a fleet of English ships appeared on the horizon, their sails billowing in the brisk wind.

Grace's jaw tightened with resolve. The moment they had prepared for had arrived sooner than expected. "Prepare for battle," she ordered, her voice carrying over the din of the crew as they scrambled into action. "We will defend our waters and our people with everything we have."

The Aoife maneuvered into position, its crew readying cannons and securing lines in anticipation of the imminent clash. Grace stood at the helm, her eyes scanning the approaching enemy fleet with steely determination. This battle was not just about defending their territory—it was a testament to their resilience and unity in the face of adversity.

As the English ships closed in, cannons thundered, filling the air with smoke and the deafening roar of battle. The Aoife rocked with the impact of enemy fire, its crew responding with precision and unwavering resolve.

Grace moved among her crew, her presence a beacon of strength and courage amidst the chaos of battle. She fought alongside them, her cutlass flashing in the sunlight as she repelled boarding attempts and rallied her crew to stand firm against the onslaught.

Amidst the fury of battle, Grace caught sight of Captain Ramirez at the helm of his own ship, leading the Spanish fleet in a coordinated assault against the English forces. Their alliance held strong, a testament to the bonds of trust and camaraderie they had forged in the crucible of conflict.

Hours passed in a blur of steel and smoke, the tide of battle shifting back and forth with each volley of cannon fire and clash of swords. The sea churned with the wreckage of fallen ships and the cries of the wounded, yet Grace O'Malley and her crew fought on with unwavering determination.

At last, as the sun dipped below the horizon and the last remnants of the English fleet retreated, a sense of victory washed over the Aoife. Cheers erupted among the crew, their voices mingling with the sounds of celebration and relief.

Grace stood at the bow of the ship once more, her eyes fixed on the darkening sea where the

English ships had disappeared into the distance. The battle had been won, but the war for Ireland's freedom was far from over.

As the stars emerged in the night sky, casting a blanket of shimmering light over the restless sea, Grace O'Malley knew that their journey was far from over. The winds of change had swept through their lives, leaving in their wake a path fraught with challenges and uncertainties.

But amidst the trials and tribulations that lay ahead, Grace remained steadfast in her resolve.

Chapter 10

Bonds, Strengthened

In the aftermath of the fierce battle against the English fleet, the Aoife sailed triumphantly back to the sheltered cove where they had often found respite and refuge. The crew, weary yet elated from their victory, worked tirelessly to repair the damages sustained during the confrontation. Amid the bustle of activity, Grace O'Malley convened a meeting with her closest advisors in the captain's quarters.

Around the worn wooden table, the atmosphere was tense yet resolute. Grace surveyed the faces of her loyal crewmates—Cormac, Captain Ramirez, and a handful of trusted allies whose unwavering loyalty had been proven time and again in the crucible of battle.

"We have emerged victorious," Grace began, her voice ringing with pride and determination.

"But our fight is far from over. The English will not rest until they have quelled our resistance and tightened their grip on our lands."

Cormac nodded in agreement, his expression serious. "Aye, Captain," he affirmed. "The battle has strengthened our resolve, but we must remain vigilant. The traitor within our ranks still lurks, and their betrayal threatens everything we have fought to protect."

Grace's jaw tightened with renewed determination. "We will root out the traitor," she declared firmly, her eyes flashing with resolve. "We cannot afford to underestimate their cunning or the threat they pose to our cause."

Captain Ramirez spoke up, his voice filled with a quiet intensity. "Grace," he began earnestly, his gaze unwavering. "I understand the gravity of the situation. I am committed to proving my loyalty to you and our alliance. Together, we will ensure that justice is served."

Grace studied him intently, her mind racing with conflicting emotions. She wanted to believe in Captain Ramirez, to trust in the bond they had forged amidst the trials and tribulations of their shared journey. But the shadows of doubt and uncertainty still lingered, a constant reminder of the dangers that surrounded them.

As they continued to strategize their next move, a commotion erupted outside the captain's quarters—a cry of alarm followed by urgent footsteps approaching from the deck. Grace and her advisors exchanged a swift glance before rushing to investigate the source of the disturbance.

On deck, they found a crew member—a young man named Liam—standing near the ship's railing, his face pale with shock and disbelief. "Captain," he stammered, his voice trembling. "You must come quickly. It's... it's the traitor."

Grace's heart clenched with a mixture of dread and determination as she followed Liam's lead. They descended below deck into the dimly lit confines of the ship's hold, where they found the captured assailant—bruised and bound, yet defiant in his silence.

"Who sent you?" Grace demanded, her voice cutting through the tense silence that enveloped them. "Who betrayed us?"

The assailant remained silent, his gaze fixed on the floor as if daring them to uncover his secrets. Grace's patience wore thin, her frustration mounting with each passing moment of silence.

"Tell us," Cormac pressed, his voice edged with urgency. "We know there are others involved. Who else is working against us?"

At last, the assailant spoke, his voice a low and chilling whisper. "You think you have won," he sneered, his lips twisting into a scornful grin. "But the real battle has only just begun."

Before Grace could react, the assailant lunged forward with unexpected strength, breaking free from his restraints and lunging for a concealed dagger. Instinct took over as Grace reacted with lightning speed, her cutlass flashing in the dim light as she deflected the assailant's blade and disarmed him once more.

The struggle was brief yet intense, the clash of steel echoing through the confined space as Grace and her crew subdued the traitor once and for all. They secured him in irons and escorted him back to the captain's quarters, where he would await justice for his crimes against their cause.

As they emerged back on deck, the air was thick with tension and unease. The traitor's revelation had shaken their confidence, yet it had also strengthened their resolve to protect their alliance and secure their freedom.

"We will interrogate him," Grace declared firmly, her voice carrying over the hushed murmurs of the crew. "We will uncover the truth and ensure that justice is served. No one will threaten our cause or our unity again."

The crew nodded in solemn agreement, their determination mirrored in their unwavering loyalty to their captain and their shared mission. As the Aoife sailed on into the night, guided by the steady rhythm of the ocean and the bonds of trust that bound them together, Grace O'Malley knew that their journey was far from over.

Amidst the challenges and uncertainties that lay ahead, she remained steadfast in her resolve to defend their homeland, forge alliances, and protect the legacy of freedom and courage that defined their fight against English tyranny.

Chapter 11

Secrets Unveiled

The Aoife sailed on through the tempestuous waters off the western coast of Ireland, its crew weary yet resolute after the recent events that had tested their loyalty and unity. Below deck, the traitor remained locked in a makeshift cell, guarded by two of Grace O'Malley's most trusted crew members. Above deck, the crew moved with a sense of purpose, their eyes scanning the horizon for any signs of trouble.

In the captain's quarters, Grace sat with Cormac and Captain Ramirez, poring over maps and discussing their next move. The atmosphere was tense, the weight of their responsibilities heavy upon them as they deliberated their strategy.

"We cannot afford to let our guard down," Cormac insisted, his voice grave with concern. "The English will not rest until they have crushed our resistance. We must remain vigilant."

Grace nodded in agreement, her mind racing with thoughts of the traitor and the shadow of betrayal that had threatened to unravel everything they had fought so hard to protect. "We need more information," she decided, her voice steady despite the turmoil within her. "We need to uncover the truth behind the traitor's motives and connections."

Captain Ramirez leaned forward, his brow furrowed with determination. "I will speak with him," he offered quietly, his voice tinged with resolve. "Perhaps I can convince him to reveal what he knows."

Grace hesitated, her trust in Captain Ramirez still tempered by the doubts that lingered in the aftermath of the betrayal. "Be cautious," she warned, her tone serious. "We cannot afford any more surprises."

As Captain Ramirez left to interrogate the traitor, Grace turned her attention to the maps spread out before her. The coastline of Ireland stretched out in intricate detail, its rugged terrain a testament to the resilience of its people and the challenges they faced in their fight for freedom.

Hours passed in tense anticipation as Grace and Cormac awaited Captain Ramirez's return. The sea churned restlessly outside, its waves crashing against the hull of the Aoife like a relentless reminder of the dangers that surrounded them.

At last, Captain Ramirez emerged from below deck, his expression grave yet determined. "He has confessed," he announced quietly, his voice barely above a whisper. "But there is more to this than we realized."

Grace and Cormac exchanged a swift glance, their curiosity piqued by Captain Ramirez's cryptic words. "What do you mean?" Grace demanded, her voice edged with urgency. "What did he tell you?"

Captain Ramirez hesitated, his gaze fixed on Grace with a mixture of concern and resolve. "The traitor revealed that he was not acting alone," he explained carefully. "He is part of a larger network—a web of deception that stretches far beyond our shores."

Grace's jaw tightened with renewed determination. "Who else is involved?" she pressed, her voice low and intense. "Who else has betrayed us?"

Captain Ramirez shook his head, his expression troubled. "He did not divulge specific names," he admitted reluctantly. "But he hinted at connections within the English court—a network of spies and informants working to undermine our efforts."

Cormac cursed under his breath, his frustration evident. "We cannot trust anyone," he muttered darkly. "Not until we uncover the extent of this conspiracy."

Grace clenched her fists, her mind racing with the implications of the traitor's revelations. "We must tread carefully," she decided, her voice tinged with determination. "We will gather intelligence, infiltrate their networks, and expose the truth behind their treachery."

As they continued to strategize their next move, a knock sounded at the door of the captain's quarters. Liam, one of the crew members who had assisted in capturing the traitor, entered cautiously.

"Captain," he began, his voice urgent. "There is something you need to see."

Curiosity piqued, Grace followed Liam out onto the deck where the crew had gathered around a figure huddled beneath a tattered cloak. As Grace approached, the figure looked up, revealing the weathered face of an elderly woman—the village seer known for her cryptic visions and unwavering connection to the ancient lore of the land.

"I have seen it," the seer declared solemnly, her voice carrying with it an air of prophecy. "The shadows of betrayal run deep, but the winds of change are coming."

Grace listened intently as the seer spoke of visions that foretold of alliances forged in fire and blood, of battles fought on distant shores, and of a destiny intertwined with the fate of Ireland itself.

"The key lies within," the seer continued, her gaze fixed on Grace with an intensity that sent a shiver down her spine. "Trust in your heart, Pirate Queen, for it holds the answers you seek."

With those enigmatic words hanging in the air, the seer turned and vanished into the night, leaving Grace and her crew to ponder the mysteries that lay ahead.

CHAPTER 12

SHADOWS OF INTRIGUE

The winds whispered secrets as the Aoife sailed onward, carrying Grace O'Malley and her crew into uncharted waters where danger lurked behind every cresting wave. The revelations from the traitor and the cryptic prophecy of the seer weighed heavily on Grace's mind, stirring a tempest of emotions within her as she navigated the turbulent seas of uncertainty.

Below deck, Captain Ramirez and Cormac continued their efforts to unravel the intricate web of betrayal that threatened their alliance and their cause. Grace sought solace in the familiar rhythms of the ship—the creak of timbers, the snap of sails, and the salty tang of the sea air that filled her lungs with each breath.

In her cabin, Grace poured over maps and scrolls, searching for clues that might shed light on the traitor's connections and the extent of the conspiracy against them. Her thoughts drifted to Captain Ramirez and the bond they had forged amidst the trials and tribulations of their shared journey.

A knock at the door interrupted her musings, and Cormac entered with a sense of urgency etched upon his weathered features. "Captain," he began, his voice grave with concern. "There has been a development."

Grace's heart quickened with anticipation as Cormac relayed the news—a messenger had arrived from a coastal village, bearing tidings of an English fleet massing on the horizon. Rumors swirled of impending reprisal for the recent defeat suffered at the hands of Grace O'Malley and her allies.

"We must prepare," Grace declared firmly, her voice tinged with steely resolve. "Gather the crew and make ready for battle. We will defend our waters and our people with everything we have."

Cormac nodded in agreement, his expression mirrored Grace's determination. Together, they rallied the crew, their voices carrying over the bustling activity as preparations for the impending confrontation intensified.

On deck, the Aoife hummed with purpose as cannons were readied, supplies secured, and defenses bolstered against the looming threat. Grace moved among her crew, her presence a calming influence amidst the mounting tension that gripped them.

As dusk descended and the first stars emerged in the night sky, the English fleet appeared on the horizon—a formidable armada of ships silhouetted against the fading light. Grace stood at the helm of the Aoife, her gaze fixed on the approaching enemy with unwavering resolve.

The air crackled with anticipation as the two fleets closed the distance, the sea swelling with the weight of history and the clash of wills that would decide the fate of Ireland's freedom. Cannons roared to life, their thunderous volleys echoing across the waves as the battle for supremacy began in earnest.

Grace fought alongside her crew, her cutlass flashing in the moonlight as she repelled boarding attempts and directed the Aoife with the skill and determination that had earned her the title of Pirate Queen. Beside her, Captain Ramirez commanded his ship with equal prowess, their alliance a beacon of unity amidst the chaos of battle.

Hours passed in a blur of smoke and steel, the ebb and flow of combat shifting with each volley of cannon fire and clash of swords. The sea churned with the wreckage of fallen ships and the cries of the wounded, yet Grace and her allies fought on with unwavering courage and determination.

As dawn broke over the horizon, the English fleet began to falter—a testament to the resilience and determination of Grace O'Malley and her crew. The remaining enemy ships turned and fled, their hopes of victory dashed against the indomitable spirit of those who fought for Ireland's freedom.

Cheers erupted among the Aoife's crew, their voices mingling with the sounds of celebration and relief as they surveyed the aftermath of the hard-won battle. Grace stood at the bow of the ship, her eyes scanning the horizon where the last remnants of the English fleet disappeared into the distance.

Amidst the jubilation and sense of triumph, Grace knew that their victory was but a temporary reprieve. The shadows of intrigue and betrayal still loomed large, casting a pall over their hard-fought triumph.

"We have prevailed," Cormac remarked, his voice tinged with exhaustion yet filled with pride. "But the traitor's network remains a threat. We must remain vigilant."

Grace nodded solemnly, her thoughts already turning to their next move. "We will gather intelligence," she decided, her voice firm with resolve. "We will uncover the truth and ensure that justice is served."

Chapter 13

The Alliance

In the aftermath of their decisive victory over the English fleet, the Aoife sailed triumphantly back to their hidden cove along the rugged Irish coast. The crew celebrated their hard-earned triumph with hearty meals, raucous songs, and tales of bravery that echoed through the night.

Grace O'Malley stood at the bow of her ship, her gaze fixed on the tranquil sea that stretched out before her. The moon cast a silvery glow over the water, illuminating the scars of battle that marred the Aoife's sturdy hull. Her mind, however, was consumed with thoughts of the traitor and the shadowy network that threatened their cause.

Cormac joined her at the railing, his presence a silent comfort amidst the quietude that enveloped them. "We cannot afford to underestimate our enemies," he remarked gravely, his eyes scanning the horizon with a wary vigilance.

Grace nodded in agreement, her expression hardened with determination. "We need allies," she asserted, her voice carrying over the gentle lapping of waves against the ship's hull. "Strong alliances that will bolster our defenses and expose the traitor's network."

Cormac considered her words thoughtfully before speaking. "There are whispers of discontent among the Irish clans," he revealed, his tone cautious yet hopeful. "Many are wary of English rule and seek to unite against their common enemy."

Grace's eyes gleamed with renewed resolve. "We will seek out these clans," she decided firmly. "We will forge alliances based on mutual respect and a shared desire for freedom."

As dawn broke over the horizon, the Aoife set sail once more, its course set for the coastal villages and strongholds of Ireland's clans. Grace and her crew navigated the intricate network of alliances and rivalries that defined the political landscape, their mission to secure support for their cause and uncover clues that would lead them closer to the heart of the traitor's conspiracy.

Their journey took them to remote villages nestled amidst rolling green hills and rocky cliffs, where they met with chieftains and warriors whose allegiance could tip the scales in their favor. Grace negotiated with a mixture of diplomacy and steely determination, her reputation as the Pirate Queen preceding her wherever she went.

In one village, they encountered Siobhan, a fierce warrior and leader of her clan, who harbored a deep-seated resentment toward English oppression. "We have suffered under their rule for too long," she declared, her voice filled with conviction. "It is time to stand together and reclaim our independence."

Grace nodded in agreement, her respect for Siobhan's resolve evident. "Together, we are stronger," she affirmed, her words echoing with the weight of their shared determination. "We will unite our forces and strike back against our common enemy."

As they forged alliances and strengthened their resolve, Grace found herself drawn to Siobhan's steadfast courage and unwavering loyalty to her people. They spent evenings strategizing by the light of campfires, their discussions filled with shared dreams of a future free from tyranny and oppression.

In the quiet moments between battles and negotiations, Grace and Siobhan found solace in each other's company—a shared understanding born of their shared struggle and their unwavering commitment to their cause.

One night, beneath a canopy of stars that shimmered like diamonds against the velvety night sky, Grace and Siobhan found themselves alone by the shore of a tranquil lake. The air was thick with anticipation as they stood facing each other, their hearts racing with unspoken desires and the weight of unspoken words.

"I have admired your courage," Grace confessed softly, her voice barely above a whisper. "You inspire me, Siobhan."

Siobhan's gaze met hers, a flicker of vulnerability beneath her stoic exterior. "And you, Grace," she replied, her voice tinged with a mixture of admiration and longing. "You have shown me what it means to lead with strength and compassion."

Their hands brushed against each other, a gentle touch that sent a shiver of electricity down Grace's spine. In that fleeting moment, amidst the turmoil of their world, they found a connection that transcended alliances and allegiances—a bond forged in the crucible of adversity and tempered by the fires of passion.

As they drew closer, their lips met in a tender kiss that spoke of longing and possibility, of shared dreams and unspoken promises. The world faded away around them, leaving only the rhythmic lullaby of the waves and the echo of their hearts beating as one.

In that timeless embrace, Grace O'Malley knew that their journey was far from over. Together with Siobhan and their newfound allies, they would continue to defy the odds, and unravel the traitor's conspiracy.

CHAPTER 14

CHANGES ON THE HORIZON

The Aoife cut through the waves with a determined grace, its sails billowing in the steady wind as it sailed toward a destiny entwined with fate. On deck, Grace O'Malley stood beside Siobhan, their hands clasped together in a silent testament to their growing bond. The past months had woven a tapestry of alliances and battles, but now, a new challenge loomed on the horizon—one that would test their resolve and shape the future of Ireland.

As they neared the shores of Connacht, rumors reached Grace of an impending English offensive aimed at crushing the growing resistance. The alliance of clans they had painstakingly forged stood united, yet the shadow of betrayal lingered like a storm cloud overhead.

Cormac approached, his expression grave with the weight of their shared burdens. "Grace," he began, his voice steady yet tinged with concern. "The English have mobilized a formidable force. We must prepare for battle."

Grace nodded, her mind already racing with strategies to defend their homeland and protect their people. "Gather the clans," she instructed firmly. "We will meet the enemy head-on and show them the strength of our resolve."

The air buzzed with anticipation as the Aoife anchored in the sheltered bay where their allies had assembled. Warriors clad in armor and wielding weapons of iron and steel stood ready, their faces set in grim determination as they awaited the inevitable clash with the English forces.

Grace addressed the gathered clans, her voice ringing out with a clarity born of conviction and defiance. "We stand together," she declared, her words echoing across the shoreline. "United in our fight for freedom and justice. Today, we defend our homeland with every fiber of our being."

A chorus of voices rose in agreement, their shouts mingling with the crash of waves and the call of seabirds wheeling overhead. With Siobhan by her side and Cormac at her back, Grace led the charge as the English ships appeared on the horizon—a formidable armada of sails and steel that bore down upon them with the fury of a storm.

Cannons roared to life, their thunderous volleys shaking the very foundations of the earth as the battle erupted in earnest. The air filled with the acrid scent of gunpowder and the cries of combatants locked in mortal struggle, their fates intertwined in the crucible of war.

Grace fought with a ferocity born of desperation and determination, her cutlass flashing in the sunlight as she repelled boarding attempts and rallied her allies to stand firm against the relentless onslaught. Beside her, Siobhan fought with a courage and skill that matched her own, their bond a beacon of hope amidst the chaos of battle.

Hours passed in a blur of smoke and steel, the ebb and flow of combat shifting with each volley of cannon fire and clash of swords. The sea churned with the wreckage of fallen ships and the cries of the wounded, yet Grace and her allies fought on with unwavering courage and determination.

As dusk settled over the blood-soaked waters, the English fleet began to falter—a testament to the resilience and unity of those who fought for Ireland's freedom. The remaining enemy ships turned and fled, their hopes of victory shattered against the indomitable spirit of Grace O'Malley and her allies.

Cheers erupted among the clans, their voices mingling with the sounds of celebration and relief as they surveyed the aftermath of the hard-won battle. Grace stood at the bow of the Aoife, her heart heavy with the weight of their sacrifices yet buoyed by the knowledge that their fight was far from over.

That night, beneath a sky ablaze with stars, Grace and Siobhan found a moment of peace amidst the chaos that had defined their lives. They stood together on the deck of the Aoife, as they gazed out over the moonlit sea.

"We have faced many challenges," Siobhan murmured softly, her voice tinged with reverence. "But together, we have overcome them all."

Grace turned to her, her eyes shining with unshed tears. "We have forged a future," she replied, her voice filled with quiet determination. "A future where our people can live in peace and freedom."

Their lips met in a tender kiss, a silent vow to stand together against whatever trials awaited them. In that fleeting moment, amidst the gentle sway of the ship and the timeless rhythm of the sea, Grace O'Malley knew that their journey had brought them to a pivotal moment—a turning point in the history of Ireland and in their own lives.

As the Aoife sailed on under the embrace of a new dawn, guided by the winds of change and the bonds of love that bound them together, Grace and Siobhan embraced the challenges that awaited them with a fierce determination and an unyielding hope for a brighter future.

CHAPTER 16

LEGACY OF THE PIRATE QUEEN

The wind whispered through the rigging of the Aoife as it sailed into the quiet harbor of Clew Bay, its hull weathered but resolute after years of battles fought and alliances forged. Grace O'Malley stood at the bow, her eyes fixed on the familiar shores of her homeland—Connacht, a land that had shaped her into the legendary figure she had become.

Behind her, Siobhan leaned against the rail, her hand resting gently on Grace's shoulder. Together, they had weathered storms both at sea and on land, their friendship strengthened by trials and triumphs that had forged a legacy beyond their wildest dreams.

As the *Aoife* docked, Grace descended onto the pier where villagers and clan leaders gathered, their faces alight with admiration and respect for the woman who had defied empires and carved a path for her people. She exchanged nods and embraces with old friends and allies, her presence a beacon of hope and inspiration.

Cormac approached, a parchment in hand that bore the seal of Connacht's clans. "Grace," he began, his voice thick with emotion. "The clans have united under your banner. They pledge their loyalty to you and to the future of Ireland."

Grace accepted the parchment with a solemn nod, her heart swelling with pride for the unity they had achieved. "Together, we are stronger," she declared, her voice carrying over the gathering crowd. "United in our commitment to freedom and justice."

Siobhan stood beside her, her gaze steady and unwavering as she surveyed the assembled clans. "We have faced many challenges," she began, her voice ringing out with quiet strength. "But our fight is not yet over."

Grace turned to Siobhan, their eyes meeting in a silent understanding of the trials that still lay ahead. "No, it is not," she agreed, her voice filled with a mixture of determination and hope.

In the days that followed, Grace O'Malley and Siobhan worked tirelessly to solidify their alliances and prepare for the challenges that awaited them. They navigated the intricate politics of Connacht, forging new alliances and strengthening old ones in their quest for a future where Ireland could thrive in peace.

But as time passed, Grace felt the weight of her years upon her. The battles had taken their toll, and she knew that her time as the Pirate Queen was drawing to a close.

Grace retired to her ancestral castle over-looking the bay, where she spent quiet moments reflecting on the journey that had brought her to this moment.

One evening, as the sun dipped low on the horizon and painted the sky in shades of gold and crimson, Grace stood on the cliffs overlooking Clew Bay. Siobhan joined her and they watched the waves crash against the rocks below.

"I have lived a life filled with adventure and purpose," Grace murmured softly, her gaze fixed on the endless expanse of the sea. "But now, it is time for a new chapter."

Siobhan nodded in understanding, her heart heavy with the knowledge that their time together as the dearest of friends would soon come to an end. "Your legacy will live on," she assured Grace, her voice filled with reverence. "In the hearts of those who fought beside you and in the stories told for generations to come."

Grace turned to Siobhan, her eyes bright with unshed tears. "And Siobhan," she whispered, her voice barely above a whisper. "You have been my anchor through storm and calm."

Siobhan pulled Grace into a sisterly embrace. In that fleeting moment, amidst the timeless beauty of Clew Bay and the echoes of their shared journey, Grace O'Malley knew that she had found her place in history—a legacy of courage, defiance, and love that would endure for eternity.

As the years passed, Grace O'Malley's legend grew, her name whispered in tales of bravery and resilience that spanned the ages. The Pirate Queen had sailed her last voyage, but her spirit lived on in the hearts of those who dared to dream of a world where freedom knew no bounds.

And as the winds carried their stories across the seas, the story of Grace O'Malley remained a beacon of hope—a testament to the enduring and indomitable spirit of a woman who had dared to defy the odds and forge her own destiny.

The Legend: Demystified

GRACE O'MALLEY:

PIRATE QUEEN

I. Early Life and Lineage (1530s-1540s)

- Born Gráinne Ní Mháille into a powerful Gaelic seafaring clan on the west coast of Ireland.
- Father: Eóghan Dubhdara Ó Máille, a chieftain and mariner.
- Learned sailing, trade, and possibly even combat from a young age.

II. Rise to Power (1540s-1560s)

- Married Dónal an Chogaidh Ó Flaithbertaigh, gaining land and influence.
- Took over leadership of the O'Malley clan after her father's death (despite having a brother).
- Engaged in piracy and trade, defending her clan's territory.
- Nicknamed "Gráinne Mhaol" (Grace O'Malley) - "Mhaol" meaning bald,

possibly due to a shaved head like a warrior.

- Possibly had a lover, a shipwrecked sailor, and avenged his death against Clan MacMahon, earning the nickname "Dark Lady of Doona."

III. Political Maneuvering (1560s-1590s)

- Ireland under English rule during her lifetime (Tudor reconquest).
- O'Malley used piracy as a political tool to challenge English dominance.
- Married secondly to Richard Bourke (Risdeard a Burca), strengthening her political and military power.
- Had four children, including sons who would continue the O'Malley legacy.

IV. The Meeting with Queen Elizabeth I (1593)

- Aimed to negotiate with the English crown for better treatment of Gaelic clans.
- Details of the meeting are unclear but became a point of legend.
- O'Malley's boldness and defiance secured some concessions for her people.

V. Later Years and Legacy (1590s-1603)

- Continued to be a powerful figure in Irish politics and maritime affairs.
- Died around 1603, a legend in her own time.
- Remembered as a pirate queen, a political leader, and a symbol of Irish resistance

  .

VI. Legacy (Beyond Death)

- Celebrated in Irish folklore, literature, and music.
- An inspiration for modern feminists and adventurers.
- Her story continues to blur the lines between fact and fiction.

THE REAL GRACE:

THE EARLY LIFE AND LINEAGE OF IRELAND'S PIRATE QUEEN

Grace O'Malley, known to history as the Pirate Queen of Ireland, remains a figure of fascination and admiration centuries after her death. Her legacy as a fearless leader, skilled sailor, and indomitable force in the face of English oppression has left an indelible mark on Irish history. Born into a seafaring family in the 16th century, Grace's early life and lineage laid the foundation for her extraordinary journey.

Grace O'Malley, or Gráinne Ní Mháille in Gaelic, was born around 1530 into Clan O'Malley, a powerful seafaring dynasty based in the rugged western coast of Ireland. The O'Malley clan, also known as the Ó Máille clan, dominated the seas of the Atlantic, controlling trade routes and engaging in both legitimate commerce and piracy. From a young age,

Grace was immersed in the maritime traditions and fierce independence that defined her clan.

Grace's father, Eoghan Dubhdara Ó Máille, was a prominent chieftain and seafarer who instilled in her a deep love for the sea and a keen understanding of navigation and maritime strategy. He recognized Grace's intelligence and determination, allowing her to accompany him on voyages and teaching her the skills necessary to command a ship—a privilege rarely granted to women in that era.

Her mother, Maeve Ní Mháille, herself a formidable figure in Clan O'Malley, further shaped Grace's upbringing. Maeve imparted the importance of clan loyalty, independence, and the resilience needed to survive in a world dominated by shifting allegiances and political intrigue.

From a young age, Grace defied societal expectations of women in 16th-century Ireland. Instead of conforming to traditional roles, she chose to embrace the freedom of the sea and the opportunities it offered. Her early experiences sailing with her father and participating in the clan's activities gave her a unique perspective on leadership and a fierce determination to chart her own course in life.

The O'Malley clan's influence extended far beyond their coastal strongholds. They held strategic alliances with other Gaelic clans and chieftains, leveraging their maritime prowess to bolster their power and prestige in the region. Grace's lineage, steeped in the rich tapestry of Irish history and mythology, imbued her with a sense of duty to her people and a desire to protect their interests against external threats, particularly from English encroachment.

Grace O'Malley's early life and lineage shaped her into the formidable leader and icon she would become—a woman ahead of her time, whose courage and determination continue to inspire generations. Her upbringing in Clan O'Malley instilled in her the values of independence, resilience, and loyalty that guided her throughout her life and defined her legacy as Ireland's Pirate Queen.

As we delve deeper into Grace O'Malley's remarkable journey, her early years stand as a testament to the enduring spirit of a woman who dared to defy convention and challenge the status quo—a legacy that resonates through the annals of Irish history and beyond.

Rise to Power

As a young woman in the 1540s, she navigated the treacherous waters of the Atlantic alongside her father, Eoghan Dubhdara Ó Máille, learning the art of seamanship and the strategies of trade and piracy that defined her family's legacy.

Grace's early ventures into maritime commerce and raiding earned her a reputation for fearlessness and cunning. She commanded her own ship and crew, challenging the notion that women were confined to domestic roles. Her exploits along the western coast of Ireland and beyond laid the groundwork for her future as a formidable leader.

During the 1550s, Grace O'Malley's influence expanded as she forged strategic alliances with neighboring Gaelic clans and chieftains. These alliances were crucial in resisting English attempts to exert control over Ireland's coastal regions. Grace's ability to navigate the complex web of Gaelic politics and maintain her clan's independence marked her as a shrewd diplomat and a respected leader.

Her command of the seas and her reputation as a fierce opponent drew admiration and respect from allies and adversaries alike. She became known as a protector of Irish interests against English encroachment, earning her the title of "Gráinne Mhaol" (Grace O'Malley) among the Gaelic clans—a name that would echo through history.

The 1560s brought heightened tensions between Grace O'Malley and English authorities, particularly under the reign of Queen Elizabeth I. Grace's refusal to submit to English dominance led to several confrontations, including a notable incident where she personally petitioned Elizabeth I for the release of her son and brother, who had been captured by English forces.

Grace's audacity in confronting the English crown and her ability to navigate the treacherous waters of Anglo-Irish relations showcased her resilience and determination. Her actions solidified her reputation as a symbol of resistance against English rule and a champion of Irish sovereignty.

As Grace O'Malley's influence grew, so too did her legend. She became a folk hero in Ireland, celebrated for her courage, leadership, and unwavering commitment to her people. Her legacy as the Pirate Queen of Ireland endures as a testament to the strength and resilience of the Gaelic clans during a tumultuous period in Irish history.

Today, Grace O'Malley's story continues to inspire artists, writers, and historians alike. Her rise to power from the 1540s to 1560s represents a pivotal chapter in the struggle for Irish independence—a testament to the enduring spirit of a woman who defied expectations, challenged authority, and forged her own path in a world dominated by men.

As we reflect on Grace O'Malley's remarkable journey, her rise to power stands as a reminder of the power of determination, leadership, and unwavering commitment to one's principles.

Political Maneuvering

In the annals of Irish history, few figures loom as large as Grace O'Malley, the legendary Pirate Queen whose political acumen and fearless leadership defined an era of resistance against English domination. From the 1560s through the 1590s, Grace navigated treacherous political waters with a mix of diplomacy, strategic alliances, and unyielding defiance—a testament to her enduring legacy as a symbol of Irish independence and resilience.

The 1560s marked a period of escalating tensions between Grace O'Malley and English authorities, particularly under the reign of Queen Elizabeth I. Grace's refusal to submit to English rule led to several confrontations, including her audacious journey to London in 1593 to petition Elizabeth I for the release of her son and brother, who had been captured by English forces.

Grace's diplomatic maneuvering during her meeting with Elizabeth I showcased her astute understanding of power dynamics and her willingness to confront authority on equal terms. Although she did not achieve all her objectives, the meeting solidified Grace's reputation as a formidable opponent and earned her grudging respect from the English court.

Throughout the 1560s to 1590s, Grace O'Malley forged and maintained strategic alliances with Gaelic clans and chieftains, as well as with European powers sympathetic to the Irish cause. These alliances were crucial in resisting English attempts to extend their control over Ireland's coastal regions and in preserving the autonomy of Gaelic culture and traditions.

Grace's ability to navigate the complex web of Gaelic politics while simultaneously engaging with European powers highlighted her diplomatic skills and strategic foresight. Her leadership extended beyond maritime exploits to include the art of negotiation and alliance-building —a testament to her multifaceted approach to defending Irish interests.

Grace O'Malley's legacy as a political leader and defender of Irish sovereignty endures to this day. Her ability to defy expectations, challenge authority, and assert Gaelic autonomy in the face of overwhelming odds inspired generations of Irish nationalists and revolutionaries. Her name became synonymous with courage, resilience, and the unwavering commitment to her people's cause.

In the centuries since her death, Grace O'Malley has been immortalized in folklore, literature, and popular culture as a symbol of Irish independence and female empowerment. Her political maneuvering during the tumultuous 1560s to 1590s remains a source of inspiration for those who continue to fight for justice, equality, and the preservation of cultural identity.

As we reflect on Grace O'Malley's political maneuvering and legacy from the 1560s to the 1590s, we are reminded of her enduring impact on Irish history and her role in shaping the course of events during a pivotal period of conflict and resistance. Her fearless leadership, diplomatic prowess, and unwavering commitment to her people's cause cemented her status as one of Ireland's most revered historical figures—a Pirate Queen whose legacy continues to inspire and captivate.

Grace O'Malley's journey from pirate to political strategist stands as a testament to the power of determination, resilience, and the unwavering pursuit of justice.

Clash of Queens

In the annals of history, certain encounters resonate as pivotal moments where the destinies of powerful individuals intersect, shaping the course of nations and leaving an indelible mark on the pages of time. One such historic meeting occurred in 1593, when Grace O'Malley, the formidable Pirate Queen of Ireland, came face to face with Queen Elizabeth I of England—an encounter that would come to symbolize the clash of two powerful women from vastly different worlds.

Grace O'Malley had risen to prominence as a fearless leader and maritime strategist, defending the interests of Gaelic clans against English encroachment along Ireland's rugged western coast. By the late 16th century, her reputation as a skilled sailor, cunning diplomat, and staunch defender of Irish autonomy had earned her respect and admiration among her allies and fear among her adversaries.

Queen Elizabeth I, on the other hand, ruled over England during a period of immense political and military challenges, including the ongoing conflict with Catholic powers in Europe and the suppression of internal dissent. Her reign was marked by efforts to consolidate English authority in Ireland, a goal that often brought her into direct conflict with Gaelic lords and chieftains like Grace O'Malley.

In 1593, Grace O'Malley embarked on a daring journey to England, determined to petition Queen Elizabeth I for the release of her son and brother, who had been captured by English forces during a skirmish. This journey was not just a diplomatic mission but a bold assertion of Grace's authority and willingness to engage with the English crown on her own terms.

Arriving in London, Grace O'Malley's presence caused a sensation at court. Clad in traditional Gaelic attire and with a retinue that included her trusted advisers and warriors, she stood out as a symbol of Gaelic resistance and independence amidst the polished sophistication of the English court.

The meeting between Grace O'Malley and Queen Elizabeth I was a clash of queens—one representing the might of the English crown, the other the resilience of Gaelic Ireland. Accounts of the encounter vary, but historical records suggest a mutual respect tinged with diplomatic tension.

Grace O'Malley, fluent in Latin and reportedly possessing a commanding presence, engaged in negotiations with Elizabeth I. Their conversation would have touched on matters of politics, sovereignty, and the treatment of Gaelic clans under English rule. Despite their differences and the disparity in their positions, the meeting highlighted Grace's determination to secure the release of her kin and to assert Gaelic rights in the face of English dominance.

The meeting between Grace O'Malley and Queen Elizabeth I resonates as a moment of defiance and diplomacy—a testament to Grace's leadership and determination to protect her people's interests. While the outcome of the negotiations is debated, the meeting itself underscored Grace's status as a formidable figure in Irish and European history—a woman who navigated the complex web of power dynamics with courage and conviction.

Grace O'Malley returned to Ireland with her son and brother freed, cementing her reputation as a leader who could challenge the might of the English crown and emerge victorious. Her legacy as the Pirate Queen who dared to confront Queen Elizabeth I continues to inspire generations, symbolizing the enduring struggle for Irish independence and the resilience of those who resist oppression.

As we reflect on the meeting between Grace O'Malley and Queen Elizabeth I in 1593, we are reminded of the power of individuals to shape history through courage, diplomacy, and a steadfast commitment to their principles. Grace O'Malley's journey to London stands as a testament to her unwavering determination to defend her people and assert Gaelic sovereignty—a legacy that continues to captivate and inspire.

In the annals of history, the meeting of Grace O'Malley and Queen Elizabeth I remains a poignant reminder of the complexities of power, identity, and resistance—a moment where two queens confronted each other across the divides of nation, culture, and history, leaving an indelible mark on the pages of time.

The Later Years

As Grace O'Malley entered her later years in the late 16th century, her commitment to defending Gaelic interests against English encroachment remained unwavering. Despite facing numerous challenges, including imprisonment and the loss of family members in skirmishes with English forces, Grace continued to lead her clan and allies in resistance.

Her strategic alliances with Gaelic chieftains and European powers sympathetic to the Irish cause bolstered her position and allowed her to navigate the complex political landscape of the time. Grace's leadership extended beyond maritime exploits to include diplomatic negotiations and strategic engagements aimed at preserving Gaelic autonomy and cultural identity.

Grace O'Malley's legacy extends far beyond her lifetime. She became a folk hero in Ireland, celebrated for her courage, determination, and unwavering commitment to her people's cause. Her name, Gráinne Mhaol, became synonymous with resilience and the fight against oppression—a testament to her enduring impact on Irish history and culture.

In the centuries following her death, Grace O'Malley's story has been immortalized in folklore, literature, and popular culture. Artists, writers, and historians continue to draw inspiration from her life and legacy, portraying her as a symbol of female empowerment and Irish nationalism. Her image adorns statues, paintings, and even modern-day representations, ensuring that her story continues to resonate with audiences around the world.

CELEBRATED LEGEND

Grace O'Malley's journey from pirate to political leader has been immortalized in countless tales passed down through generations. In Irish folklore, she is often depicted as a fearless warrior queen, navigating treacherous waters and outwitting her enemies with cunning and bravery. Her encounters with mythical creatures and supernatural beings further embellish her legend, portraying her as a figure of almost mythical stature.

These folktales, while embellished with elements of fantasy, reflect the deep reverence and admiration for Grace O'Malley among the Irish people. Her exploits have become part of the cultural fabric, inspiring stories of resistance and heroism that continue to captivate audiences of all ages.

Grace O'Malley's story has also left an indelible mark on Irish literature, where she is celebrated as a symbol of female empowerment and Irish nationalism. Writers and poets have drawn inspiration from her life, crafting narratives that explore themes of identity, rebellion, and the struggle against oppression.

In contemporary literature, Grace O'Malley appears as a complex and multifaceted character, challenging conventional portrayals of women in history. Authors have reimagined her adventures, delving into her motivations, relationships, and the impact of her leadership on Irish society. Through these literary works, Grace O'Malley's story continues to evolve, resonating with readers who seek to uncover the truth behind the legend.

The legacy of Grace O'Malley extends into Irish music, where she is immortalized in ballads and songs that celebrate her courage and defiance. Traditional Irish musicians have composed melodies that recount her daring escapades, capturing the spirit of adventure and rebellion that defined her life.

These musical tributes often blend historical accounts with poetic license, creating a narrative that reflects both the harsh realities of Grace's time and the romanticized allure of her persona. From haunting laments to spirited sea shanties, the music inspired by Grace O'Malley evokes a sense of nostalgia for Ireland's maritime heritage and a deep-seated pride in her role as a national icon.

The enduring fascination with Grace O'Malley lies in the blurred lines between fact and fiction surrounding her life. Historical records provide glimpses into her achievements and challenges, yet much of her story remains shrouded in mystery and embellishment. This ambiguity has allowed her legend to transcend time, evolving with each retelling to reflect the values and aspirations of different generations.

While historians strive to uncover the truth behind the myth, the allure of Grace O'Malley as a symbol of resistance and female empowerment continues to grow. Her story resonates with audiences who are drawn to tales of bravery and defiance against overwhelming odds—a testament to her enduring legacy in Irish folklore, literature, and music.

Grace O'Malley, the Pirate Queen of Ireland, stands as a testament to the power of myth and the enduring appeal of stories that transcend generations. Celebrated in folklore, literature, and music, her legacy continues to inspire and captivate, blurring the lines between fact and fiction to remind us of the timeless ideals of courage, resilience, and the fight for freedom.

As we continue to unravel the layers of Grace O'Malley's story, her journey serves as a beacon of hope and empowerment for all who dare to challenge the status quo and forge their own path in the world—a legacy that will continue to echo through the ages.

IF YOU'VE ENJOYED THIS BOOK,

Please consider leaving an honest review at your favorite online book retailer. It's like sending a cookie to the author without having to spend a penny.

www.ingramcontent.com/pod-product-compliance
Lightning Source LLC
Chambersburg PA
CBHW051220160726
47994CB00002B/680